KiNG
FLASHYPANTS
AND THE TOYS OF TERROR

HODDER CHILDREN'S BOOKS

First published in Great Britain in 2017 by Hodder and Stoughton

1 3 5 7 9 10 8 6 4 2

A CIP catalogue record for this book is available from the British Library.

ISBN 978 1 444 92961 4

Designed by Jennifer Stephenson
Edited by Emma Goldhawk

Printed and bound in Great Britain by CPI Group (UK) Ltd,
Croydon, CR0 4YY.

The paper and board used in this book are from well-managed forests and
other responsible sources.

MIX
From responsible
sources
FSC® C104740

Hodder Children's Books
An imprint of Hachette Children's Group
Part of Hodder & Stoughton
Carmelite House, 50 Victoria Embankment
London EC4Y 0DZ

An Hachette UK Company
www.hachette.co.uk

www.hachettechildrens.co.uk

KING FLASHYPANTS

AND THE TOYS OF TERROR

h

Hodder
Children's
Books

WRITTEN AND DRAWN BY ANDY RILEY

With thanks to
Polly Faber, Bill Riley, Eddie Riley,
Emma Goldhawk, Jennifer Stephenson,
Anne McNeil, Gordon Wise,
Hilary Murray Hill, Lucy Upton,
Stephanie Allen, Jennifer Breslin,
Emily Thomas, Kevin Cecil,
Greta Riley and Robin Riley

Dedicated to Daisy Wilson

KING EDWIN
FLASHYPANTS

MINISTER JILL

MEGAN THE JESTER

EMPEROR NURBISON

THE OLD EMPRESS VERONICA

GLOBULUS

Just imagine how Exciting all these chapters must be

The Ninth of Janvember

Long, long ago, there was a time called 'the olden days'. The olden days came before nowadays, which is when we live. But it came *after* 'the olden olden days', when everybody lived in caves and spoke in grunts and hit each other with clubs all day.

OLDEN OLDEN DAYS

OLDEN DAYS

NOWADAYS

The olden days was a time of magic and monsters and knights and castles. And in one of those castles there lived a nine-year-old boy. His name was King Edwin Flashypants, and he was about to hide inside a box of cornflakes.

If you try this in your kitchen, you won't fit, unless you've just shrunk to the size of a pencil case, and if you have then please see a doctor right away. But Edwin was a king, so he had a

giant packet specially made for banquets. It was as big as a mattress.

His friends gave him a leg-up. He tumbled inside with a **FLUMP-SCRUNCH**, and poked two holes in the cardboard so he could see out.

"She'll be waking up soon!" said Edwin. "Everybody hide, quick as you can!"

Edwin's pals hurried around the castle's kitchen.

Minister Jill, the grown-up who helped Edwin with the difficult bits of running a kingdom, crawled into a sack of potatoes.

Centurion Alisha and her palace guards hid
among the pots and pans.

Baxter the hermit, whose beard was longer than he was, did a headstand in a vase. He was pretending to be a pot plant.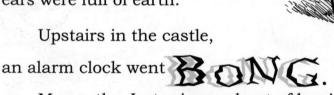

"Baxter, she'll see you there for sure," said King Edwin, but Baxter couldn't hear because his ears were full of earth.

Upstairs in the castle, an alarm clock went **BONG**.

Megan the Jester jumped out of her jester-shaped bed. She checked the calendar.

"The ninth of Janvember!" said Megan. *"It's my birthday!"*

She was so excited she slid down all the
banisters in the castle, knocking over Minister
Jill's signs which said *Please Don't Slide
Down The Banisters.* Then she ran to the
kitchen, where she knew that
Edwin and all her friends
would be waiting to give
her a special birthday
breakfast.

But the
kitchen was quiet.

"Nobody here,"
said Megan.

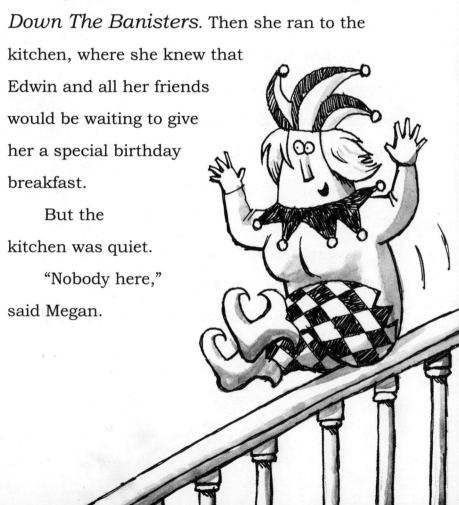

"Everything's normal, except for that weird hairy plant on the table."

She slumped down on the potato sack. For a second, she thought she heard a potato say "ouch".

"I suppose I'll have to make my *own* birthday breakfast," sighed Megan.

She hefted the giant box of cornflakes off the counter. It seemed heavier than normal. Then she tipped it over her favourite bowl. Out came a thousand cornflakes – and a nine-year-old king.

"Surprise!" shouted Edwin.

"SURPRISE!" shouted everybody else, as they jumped out from their hiding places.

"You did remember, you did, you did!" said Megan. She couldn't be happier.

"And now for the birthday presents!" said Edwin.

Centurion Alisha and the other palace guards gave Megan a pogo stick.

"It's a pogo stick," said Centurion Alisha.

"Thanks – oOf! Just what I – oOf! – wanted – oOf!" said Megan,

9

who was already pogo-ing her head into the kitchen ceiling.

"I wasn't sure what you'd like, so I thought I'd give you the money," said Minister Jill. There are some grown-ups who always do that, and Jill was one of them.

Baxter gave Megan a single glove, and promised that if she wore it a lot, he would buy her a matching one next year.

"I've *made* you a present," said King Edwin. "Just close your eyes, Megan ..."

Megan closed her eyes. She hoped it was

going to be as wonderful as a pogo stick, money
or a single glove.

"Open them!" said Edwin.

Megan looked. There was a mirror in front
of her - and in the mirror, Megan saw she was
wearing a hat made from
a cardboard box. Paper
lightning bolts
were held on
with sticky
tape.

There was a cape made from duvet covers round her shoulders. Edwin looked just as strange. What was this all about?

"Hope you like my present, Megan. It's an idea I've had. We're going to play

SUPERHEROES!"

Because this was the olden days, and Edwin was the first person to ever think of superheroes, he had to explain what they were.

"Superheroes have costumes and exciting names, and they go around fighting baddies and saving the world with their super powers!"

"Are super powers like magic powers?" said Megan.

"No," said Edwin. "Super powers are different. They're *super*."

Nobody quite understood the difference, but because Edwin was the king, everyone nodded as if they did.

Edwin handed Megan some Hero Information Cards with everything she needed to know.

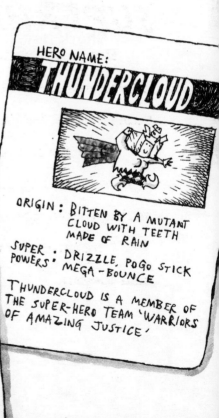

HERO NAME:

THUNDERCLOUD

ORIGIN: BITTEN BY A MUTANT CLOUD WITH TEETH MADE OF RAIN

SUPER POWERS: DRIZZLE, POGO STICK MEGA-BOUNCE

THUNDERCLOUD IS A MEMBER OF THE SUPER-HERO TEAM 'WARRIORS OF AMAZING JUSTICE'

HERO NAME:

SHARK BOY

ORIGIN: ONE DAY, JUST DECIDED SHARKS WERE AWESOME

SUPER POWERS: JUDO, SHARK TICKLE

SHARK BOY IS A MEMBER OF THE SUPER-HERO TEAM 'WARRIORS OF AMAZING JUSTICE'

Minister Jill thought: *clouds don't have teeth. And sharks can't tickle. This is nonsense. No, I think Megan would have liked a better present, like a nice vase or some light brown socks or ...*

"I love it!" said Megan. "Hey Shark Boy, let's play superheroes!"

First, they all ate a really special birthday
breakfast, with treats like eggs
made out of sausage, and
sausages made out of
egg. Then King Edwin
and Megan the Jester
played superheroes for
the rest of the morning.
They saved the world
from alien invaders and
mechanical monsters.

Think of the best playtime you've ever had
with your favourite friend. Now imagine
that day, but in a big castle full
of slides and tunnels and trap
doors. That was the day
Edwin and Megan had.

"Imagine
if Warriors of
Amazing Justice
had to fight *real*
villains," said
Edwin.

"But the only baddie round here is Emperor Nurbison, and I don't think he'll try anything again," said Megan.

"Haha! Not since we beat him twice, no!"

"We're totally safe forever," said Megan.

For a second, Edwin wondered if being a bit more worried about Emperor Nurbison would be a good thing for a king to do.

Then he thought, *let's go and eat chips.*

The Cottage and the Cupboard

Emperor Nurbison was all about the hating. Hating was his hobby. He loved to hate stuff, and he hated to love stuff.

He hated white cats, because they ran away whenever he tried to stroke them, even though villains are *supposed* to stroke white cats. He hated rainbows because their pretty colours cheered everybody up. He hadn't yet found a way to chop rainbows down when they appeared, even though he had tried lots of times with a big axe. He hated King Edwin Flashypants most of all, because Edwin stopped him from invading the annoyingly happy and un-hatey place called Edwinland.

The list of things Emperor Nurbison actually *liked* was very short. There wasn't much on it except 'being evil' and 'pointy boots'.

But even the evillest emperors have to go and visit their mum sometimes.

Nurbison's mum was called Veronica, and she was once an evil empress feared around the world. Then her knees went. So she retired to a little cottage by the sea with roses climbing all round the front door. Veronica being as evil as she was, they were man-eating roses.

"Globulus!

To my side!" said the emperor, and his loyal
assistant scurried forward.

"I don't want those roses nipping at my
handsome beard when I go in," said the emperor.
"But they won't bother me if they're
busy chomping your face
off, will they, Globulus?"

"You know, like, well,
thing is," said Globulus,
"them roses are proper
scary, kind of thing,
so I—"

The emperor rolled
Globulus at the roses.

Globulus was the size and shape of a bowling ball, so this wasn't too hard.

Globulus bumped into the biggest flower. It didn't even twitch.

"Good!" said the emperor. "They must be asleep."

Nurbison strode straight for the door. Five roses gnashed him with their thorny jaws.

After leaving Globulus to fight the roses –
and after realising he could have gone in
through the back door – the emperor was in the
cottage, having tea with his mother.

"Can I tempt you with a biscuit, my darling
Nurbly-Nibs?" said Empress Veronica, holding out
a tray.

'DEAD STARFISH'
BISCUIT, MADE
FROM A DEAD
STARFISH

TRIPLE DECKER
CHOCOLATE COOKIE
WITH WHITE
CHOCOLATE CHIPS

RANCID
NINE-YEAR-OLD
WAFER

DRIED POND
SLIME BISCUIT
WITH A ROTTEN
CHERRY ON THE TOP

SNOTGESTIVE

Nurbison took the chocolate cookie with white chocolate chips. When he bit into it, he discovered the white chocolate chips were really maggots. If you've ever seen dogs wriggle through a line of poles at a dog display – that's what the little creatures were doing round the emperor's teeth.

"Thank you, Mother," Nurbison muttered.

"Ha! Ha! Ha! The old maggoty biscuit prank! Not very dastardly I know, but it's the best I can do at my age," said Veronica. "So, son, you're an evil emperor – what kind of evilness have you been up to?"

"What evilness *haven't* I been up to, more like! **FOO HOO HOO HOO**, Mother,

FOO HOO HOO HOO!"

'Foo hoo hoo hoo' was Emperor
Nurbison's evil laugh. It could even scare
things that don't normally get scared, like
tigers or loaves of bread. But no matter how
hard he tried – and he *was* trying
– he wasn't sure it
was working on
his mum.

"Ah, the horrors I have unleashed upon this world!" said Emperor Nurbison. "I poured salt into a sugar bowl, ruining several mugs of tea! I made a pigeon cry by calling it Stumpy Toes! I glued a penny to the pavement, then watched people try to pick it up! Truly, my wickedness knows no bounds! And then I—"

"**PAH!**" said Veronica. "That's not evil, that's just a bit naughty. A *truly* evil emperor wouldn't get beaten – twice! – by Edwin Flashypants. You can't even seize a kingdom from a little boy!"

The emperor looked at his shoes. Mum had a point.

"Back in the day, son," said Veronica, "I would have mashed him to paste. Then fed the paste to the wolves. Then blown up the wolves."

She struggled out of her chair, rummaged in a dark cupboard, and pulled out a picture in a grimy old frame. She blew the dust off, making sure to get most of it in Emperor Nurbison's face.

"Quite something when I was young, wasn't I?" she said. "Sword as long as a giraffe's trousers. Eye-patch, even though both my eyes were perfectly fine. Kept bumping into things but oh, I looked terrifying! The things I got up to ..."

Emperor Nurbison had heard this speech before. He wasn't looking at the picture. He was staring at something which had tumbled out of the cupboard as the empress had been rummaging. Something he hadn't seen since he was a small child.

A doll.

Years ago, when Nurbison was a boy, his
mother had kept it on a shelf. It had beautiful
black shiny hair, and big gleaming eyes. He
used to find it a bit scary.

"... so I boiled the king of the Ant-People
with hot water from a massive kettle, and then
... Nurbison, why are you staring at that useless
old magic doll?"

"It's magic? Didn't know that," said
Emperor Nurbison, yawning as if he wasn't
very interested. Really, he was very interested
indeed.

"Got her from a wizard when I was a girl,"
said Veronica. "He gave her enchanted hair.

When the rays of the full moon touch the hair, she comes to life for a year and a day. But when she does, oh! She just talks about her hair. All the time. Just banging on and on and on. Soon learned to keep her out of the moonlight, I can tell you. She's called Miss Dolly-Chops, or something. Only kept her on show because I knew she frightened you."

Old Empress Veronica tossed the picture and the doll back in the cupboard.

"Beloved Mother," said Nurbison, "Empress of my heart. Why don't you sit back in your chair and rest those knees of yours, while I put the biscuits back in the kitchen?"

"I know what you're up to," said Veronica. "Snaffling an extra biccie. Try and there'll be trouble, young man."

"Mother, I promise I shall not steal a single biscuit."

I'm not lying, thought Nurbison. *I'm not going to steal any biscuits at all. I'm going to steal something else.*

Once he was sure his mum wasn't looking, the emperor eased open the cupboard door, hoping it wouldn't creak. He found the doll and stuffed it inside his cloak. Big swirling cloaks are just the best for hiding stuff you nicked.

Yes, this magic doll will be very useful,

thought Emperor Nurbison. *Very useful indeed. I feel a plan forming in my evil genius brain.*

He didn't dare say Foo Hoo Hoo Hoo in case his mother figured out he was up to something. So he wrote it down on a piece of paper, looked at it, smiled, then ate the paper. It was tastier than the biscuit.

A Month Later

It was a month later.

King Edwin sat on his throne, picking scabs off his knees. It had been three whole days since King Edwin's last amazing invention – the skateboard. He made two of them, so Shark Boy and Thundercloud could have one each. But he hadn't invented knee pads yet.

Something was strange. Minister Jill wasn't
telling him to stop picking.

"Jill? You're forgetting to say 'leave the
scabs on, they help your skin to heal'. I could
say it for you if I like. Oh wait, I just did."

"I'm not really thinking about your scabs,
Edwin – I'm thinking about Emperor Nurbison.
He's been acting a bit odd."

That was true. Three weeks before, he had marched up to the dotted line between Edwinland and Nurbisonia, and instead of calling Centurion Alisha a foolish fool, or just invading, he'd said:

I JUST **LOVE** THAT 'CLANKY ARMOUR' LOOK. IT'S SO... **YOU.**

A few days after that, the emperor had started wearing a big yellow daisy in his crown. Then he'd let his peasants have a proper wash. Which was strange, because normally the emperor loved his peasants to be filthy and miserable, and made them wash their hair with slug juice and brush their teeth with dog sweat.

"There's just something peculiar about it all," said Minister Jill.

A palace guard popped out of a trap door in the floor. There were so many trap doors and secret passages in Edwin's castle that it was a wonder there was any space left for actual rooms.

"Your majesty! Minister Jill! The Nurbisonia Times. Just delivered. One copy for each of you."

Jill and Edwin looked at each other in amazement. Nurbisonia had a newspaper now? The Evil Emperor was letting people *read*?

First, Jill made herself a big cup of coffee. Most grown-ups need coffee five times a day or they turn into zombies. Just ask them.

Then Jill sat down with the paper. The front page had some very big news.

Jill flicked to the next page.

Nurbisonia Times

4TH OF OCTEBRUARY ∾ PRICE : 2 BRONZE BITS

"I'M NICE NOW!"

- ALL CHANGE FOR THE NOT-SO-EVIL EMPEROR
- FULL STORY : PAGES 1, 2, 3, 4, 5, 6, 7, 8, 9, 10, 11, 12, 13, 14, 15, 16, 17, 18

A NEW NURBISON?

THE BIG INTERVIEW,

BY OUR CHIEF REPORTER

After years of being popular and strong and handsome, but also utterly evil, it seems our great emperor's had a change of heart about the whole 'evil' thing. We caught up with him in his stunning castle penthouse to find out more ...

THE TIMES: So! Emperor Nurbison, Earl of Unjerland, Overlord of Glenth and Boolander ...

EMPEROR NURBISON: (waving his hand) Oh, you don't have to call me by those fancy titles every time. I see myself as a … how do people say it? A 'regular guy'.

THE TIMES: I'll tell you what else people are saying … 'Emperor, why the big change?'

EMPEROR: I'm so glad you asked me that. I used to be very evil indeed. Then I was defeated twice in a row by my delightful neighbour King Edwin Flashypants. Wonderful little chap, love him to death. So I thought to myself: why does he keep winning? Is good better than evil after all?

On that day I decided to become a nice emperor. **FOO HOO**— oh, sorry. That was my old evil laugh. You won't be hearing that any more. I've got a new jolly laugh now. **SQUEE HEE HEE HEE!** Like it?

THE TIMES: I do. **SQUEE HEE HEE HEE!** Wow, it's very catchy.

THE ~~EVIL~~ HANDSOME EMPEROR RELAXES IN HIS DEEPLY ~~SINISTER~~ NICE HOME

EMPEROR: And I won't stop there. In my evil years I caused a lot of misery. From now on, I'll spread all the happiness I can. I'm becoming a toymaker. I'm turning the castle into a big toy factory. I'll sell the toys in my new toyshops, and with luck … where I once brought sadness … I can bring just a little bit of joy. Sniff.

EDITOR'S NOTE: AT THIS MOMENT, A TEAR REALLY DID RUN DOWN OUR EMPEROR'S BEAUTIFUL FACE!

THE TIMES: Good luck, Emperor. We can't wait for the first shop to open!

"What do you make of all that?" said Minister Jill to King Edwin.

"Make of what?" said Edwin, "The news? Oh, I don't look at news, it's never fun. But there's comic strips at the back, look. This one's called Mister Poo and it's about a poo who lives in a house made of poo! You'd enjoy it Jill, the jokes are very clever."

Jill held the headline under Edwin's
nose.

"Nurbison's NICE?" said the king.
"That IS big news. Why did they hide it on the
front page?"

The sky went dark. There was a
thundering sound on the roof, like the heaviest
rain King Edwin had ever heard.

But it wasn't rain.

"Newspapers!" said Jill.

High above Edwinland, hundreds of the
emperor's crows were dropping copies of the
Nurbisonia Times. Everybody in Edwinland
picked one up and read it.

Seconds later, Megan the Jester burst

into the throne room. She pulled off her

Thundercloud hat and cape.

"Have you seen it? Have you? Have you seen it? Have you seen it? Have you? Have you seen it? Have you? Have you? Have you seen it?" said Megan, breathless. "The emperor's going to make toys! So many toys. I love toys! Can we go to the toyshop as soon as it opens? **Please? Please?**"

When people get older, most of them forget just how cool toys are. That's just one of the things which makes grown-ups more boring than kids. But even though she was a grown-up, Megan never forgot, and Edwin loved her for it.

"Well, Emperor Nurbison *is* good now, I suppose ..." said Edwin.

"He's pretended to be nice before, then turned out to be horrible," said Jill.

"But he never pretended for more than an hour. If it seems like he's been good for a whole month – maybe he really **is** good. *Maybe.* We'd better give him a chance, at least."

"Megan," said King Edwin, "we'll go to the toyshop."

"Hooray! Yay! Woo-hoo! All the other words like that!" said Megan. Then she ran upstairs to see how much was in her money box.

Megan forgot to pick up her Thundercloud cape, thought King Edwin. *And the helmet got a bit bashed up when she dropped it. But I know she loves it, so I'll find some sticky tape and fix it for her.*

He picked up the newspaper and looked at the comic strips again. Mister Poo was wearing a poo for a hat and walking his pet poo, when he tripped over a poo and fell in some poo. It was just the kind of thing Edwin liked. But he wasn't laughing as much as he normally would.

Something was worrying him about Megan. But what was it?

51

Grand Opening

For the next few nights, Nurbison's peasants hammered and sawed and built, saying things like "let's lay some bricks here" and "where shall I put the floorboards?" and "on the floor, dummy". In just a few days, there was a shiny new toy shop at the edge of Nurbisonia, just by the dotted line.

The crows flapped over Edwinland again, dropping paper scrolls which said:

EMPEROR NURBISON'S TOY SUPERSTORE

GRAND OPENING:
SATURDAY, 12 NOON
"A GREAT BIG FUN SANDWICH OF A SHOP!"

Before the sun even rose on Saturday morning, King Edwin Flashypants was woken by a great big jester trampolining on his bed.

"Let's be first in the queue!" said Megan. "Let's! Let's! Let's!"

But when they got there, there was already a great snaking line of people in front of the superstore. The people of Edwinland couldn't wait to see what was inside.

"Your Majesty! You should come to the front of the queue," said one peasant.

"You are the king after all," said another.

"Thanks, but I think I'll wait like everyone else," said King Edwin. "Just because I'm royal doesn't mean I should jump the line."

When she heard this, Minister Jill felt
incredibly proud. She turned to tell Edwin he
was growing into a very wise and mature king,
but Edwin had already started a bogey-flicking
contest with some other children.

All morning, the people waited.

The sun crept across the sky, stayed

10
POINTS

still for a bit just to annoy everyone, then crept a little more.

"Hey, Megan," said King Edwin. "Let's pretend there's a dinosaur, which is also a zombie and also a Dracula. A dino-zomb-cula! And it's attacking this queue! But wait, here come Thundercloud and Shark Boy!"

Megan didn't even look his way.

"Megan? Megan. Megan. Megan. Megany-Megan. *Megaaaaaaaaaaaaaaaaaaan.*"

"I wonder if they do a discount for jesters?" said Megan, gazing at the superstore.

At seven seconds before
twelve, Globulus popped out of a
hatch on top of the shop.

"I kind of like, you know, sort of,
declare this superstore kind of open,
sort of thing!" said Globulus.

That meant the superstore was open.

Everybody hurried inside. The shop was
simply enormous. The shelves seemed to go on
forever. But wherever he walked, Edwin noticed
the toys had one thing in common.

"They're all Emperor Nurbison dolls," he said.

"I know!" said Megan. "And so many
different kinds!"

NURBISON
CLASSIC

DEEP SEA DIVER
NURBISON

CHEF NURBISON

FUNKALICIOUS
NURBISON

She was right.

BURGER AND
FRIES NURBISON

COWGIRL
NURBISON

RETARIUS
GLADIATOR
NURBISON

WITH TRIDENT!

NANNY
NURBISON

And lots and lots more.

Hundreds of different Nurbisons.

EXPLORER
NURBISON

PRINCESS
NURBISON

For boys who thought buying a doll was a bit girly, there was another part of the shop where they sold all the same stuff, but under a big sign which said **'ACTION FIGURES'**.

"Nurbison is such a big-head!" said King Edwin, who was secretly a bit jealous he hadn't been the first to think of making dolls of himself.

Megan chose a Princess Nurbison doll and followed the 'This Way To Pay' signs. Emperor Nurbison worked the giant till, which played jolly pipe music whenever he made a sale.

"Such merriment! Enjoy your toys, everyone!" said the emperor. "Oh, hello King Edwin, so glad you could come! SQUEE HEE HEE HEE!"

After banging the till's huge buttons for a while, the emperor announced his arms

SALE SALE SALE

BAGS
5p

were tired. "But never mind!" he said. "One of my sinister— I mean, *un*-sinister soldiers will take over."

Nurbison and Globulus stepped out of the back door. The moment they were alone, the emperor's smile collapsed into a scowl.

"It's infernally hard work, pretending to be good," said Nurbison. "I've never kept it up for this long before. And this false beard is giving me a rash."

The emperor pulled a fake beard from his chin. He'd had a shave. *In secret.*

"Just, you know, a few more days, your sensationalness," said Globulus, slapping moisturiser on the Emperor's bare face.

"Yes!" said Nurbison. "And then all shall
know the true might of the Evil Emperor
Nurbison!"

Then the emperor had to fetch a mop and
bucket, because a baby had just been sick in
aisle number five.

Big Pouty Face

Bang, bang, bang. Bang, bang. Ba-ba-bang. Bang. Ba-bang. Bang, bang, bang, ba-ba-ba-ba-ba-bang.

Bang, bang, Ba-bang.

Ba-bangbangbangbangbangbang.

Bang.

Shark Boy was knocking on Thundercloud's bedroom door.

Edwin had just put a cool tail on the Shark

Boy hat. It took lots and lots of sticky tape to

keep it in place, and he was very proud of it.

"Megan! My lessons are over! Let's play

superheroes! *Megaaaaan!*"

There was no reply. Edwin jumped on to a giant boingy spring. Giant boingy springs were another cool way to get around inside the castle. It boinged him all the way up to the battlements.

He gazed across Edwinland. It seemed like everybody was carrying Emperor Nurbison dolls.

And there was Megan, by the castle moat. It looked like playing superheroes couldn't be further from her mind. Edwin frowned as he watched her dancing her princess

Nurbison all about, and singing a song to it.

Something like this:

Here's a little ditty
    To tell you you're so pretty.
A princess with a silky beard so fine
    You really are so nice
And at such a modest price
You retailed for just seven ninety-nine.

King Edwin called Centurion Alisha. She
clanked towards him in her steel armour, then
stamped her feet so hard a chunk of the ceiling
shook loose in the room below and hit Minister
Jill on the head.

"Your Majesty!" said Centurion Alisha.

"Alisha? If anybody needs me, I'll be
in my throne room having a massive sulk,"
said Edwin.

Kings never have small sulks. Edwin
really threw himself into this one, doing all
the things nine-year-olds do when they're in
a bad mood.

He pouted until his face got tired.

He sat in his throne the wrong way round with his feet sticking in the air.

He pouted some more.

He kicked his foot with his other foot.

He moaned and sighed and banged things with a stick.

It's not fair, he thought. *Megan is my best friend and she doesn't want to play superheroes with me any more. She just wants to play with her stupid Nurbison doll like everybody else.*

Normally, Megan was there to cheer Edwin up when he was like this. But today, Megan was the reason *why* he was like this.

In came Minister Jill, rubbing the bump on her head.

"Something's wrong about all this," said Jill.

"Mumble mumble mumble," mumbled Edwin, because when you're mega moody it's important to speak like that.

"We've let Emperor Nurbison sell toys to everyone in Edwinland," Jill continued. "And it's good that we did, because we said we'd give him a chance to be nice ..."

Minister Jill took a deep breath, then puffed her cheeks out.

Edwin checked the list of Jill's moves he kept under his throne pillow. Puffy cheeks meant that Jill's next word would be 'but'.

"But," said Jill, "Just say he *wasn't* nice. Then the toys could be part of some new plan of – well, how can I say this – *not-niceness*."

73

Megan bounced into the throne room, and the wind blew a hundred new toy catalogues through the door after her. Nurbison's crows had been dropping them for the last hour. They fell so thick in some places that the shorter peasants were stuck up to their necks.

"There's a new Princess Nurbison play set!" Megan gasped. "It's got an ice-cream parlour and a beard salon, look!"

She held two catalogues in front of King Edwin's face, one for each eye. Then Megan the Jester ran up to her bedroom,

grabbed some gold coins
from her money-box,
and dashed out to the
superstore.

"Maybe we should take a
really close look at
a Nurbison doll," said Minister Jill.
"Even though I'm absolutely sure
there's nothing to worry about."

"Oh, I know where to find one of
those," said King Edwin.

And he climbed the stairs.

All the way to Megan's
bedroom.

Find The Princess

As he pushed open Megan's bedroom door, Edwin thought, *I'm just borrowing her doll, not stealing it. And while I know that's not quite true, if I keep saying it in my head I might start to believe it. I'm borrowing, not stealing. Borrowing, not stealing.*

Since the last time
Edwin was in Megan's room,
she had built a massive
play castle on the floor out
of old toys and games. The
Princess Nurbison doll was
perched right on top.

Wow. You could stack seven of me up the side of that thing, thought Edwin. *Hey! If I had six identical brothers, you really could stack up seven of me, and we could be a circus act. The Flying Flashypants-es! And we'd wear spangly cat-suits and we'd flip into the big top like this ...*

King Edwin tried a cartwheel, stabbed his left hand with his crown, tumbled to the floor, and nudged the play castle.

It creaked and rocked – but didn't come crashing down on Edwin.

It really **wobbled** *a lot then,* thought Edwin. *But it didn't ACTUALLY come crashing down on my head so I reckon it's totally safe to climb.*

Edwin clambered up the princess's castle. When he couldn't find the next handhold, he opened up board games and looked for useful things inside the boxes. Hooky Duck had a tiny fishing rod. With a bit of hook-throwing and bit of reel-winding, Edwin climbed higher still.

At the top, the king grabbed the princess doll

with his teeth and climbed all the way down again.

Whew! Not so hard, thought Edwin, leaning against the play castle's biggest tower.

The castle groaned, rumbled and toppled over.

Edwin ran.

I'm not going to get crushed, he thought. *Going to make it to the door ... just in time ...*

Just ... in ... time ...

Seventy jigsaws landed on his head. Alisha and the palace guards had to use every single rod from Hooky Duck to pull him out.

Later, down in the throne room, Jill and Edwin looked at the Princess Nurbison doll this way, then that way. Then sideways, topways and underways.

"Just a normal-looking doll," said Edwin.

"Well, nothing weird about the outside," said Jill. "So maybe there's something *inside* it."

King Edwin was still pretty sure Emperor Nurbison was nice these days. *But if he wasn't,* Edwin thought, *what might he hide inside a doll ...?*

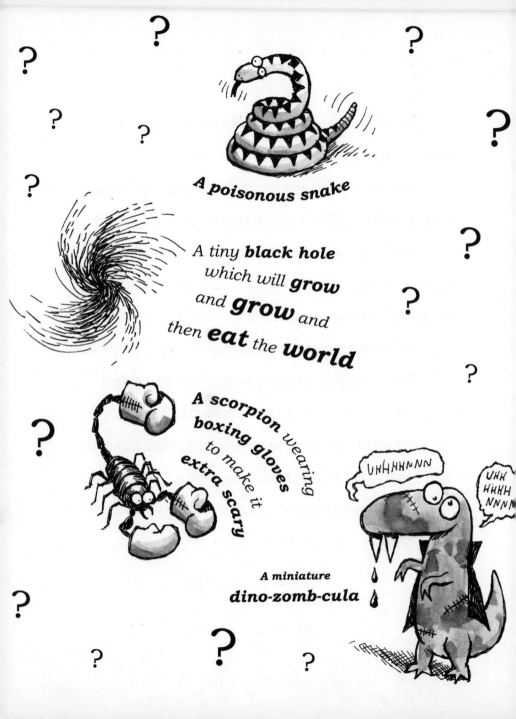

Just the thought of that last one made Edwin's blood run cold.

"We have to open it up and find out," said King Edwin. "Jill? The big tongs, please."

Jill fetched a couple of pairs of tongs from a big fireplace. Edwin gripped Princess Nurbison's head with one pair and Jill held Princess Nurbison's feet with the other.

Megan really really really really wouldn't like this, thought Edwin. *But if I fix the doll straight afterwards, she'll never know.*

"One, two—" said Jill.

"Wait," said Edwin. "Let's count down, not up. Down sounds cooler."

"Oh, all right then," said Minister Jill.

"Three, two, one – pull!"

They both heaved. With a pop, then a rip,

the Princess Nurbison doll broke in two.

Edwin and Jill each looked at their own part.

"Just wood and wire and cotton stuffing in my bit," said Jill.

"Same here," said Edwin.

"WHAT HAVE YOU DONE?!"

said Megan the Jester.

Jill and Edwin looked up. There she was, clutching her new Princess Nurbison playset. They hadn't heard her come in.

"You've broken Princess
Nurbison! You rotten snot-
lords, you snapped her
in half!"

"Well ... well ... who
cares about a stupid Princess
Nurbison doll anyway? They
all belong in the bin!" said Edwin.

"Megan, Edwin. Let's just calm down," said
Minister Jill. "Before we all say a lot of angry
words we won't be proud of later."

But Edwin and Megan weren't listening.
They were too busy saying lots of angry words
they wouldn't be proud of later.

"*I* care!" said Megan. "She was my favourite toy and you're just jealous because ... because ... because ...

YOUR SUPERHERO COSTUMES ARE RUBBISH!"

"They are not!" said King Edwin.

"They are so!" said Megan. "They're not even made properly, they've got lots of sticky tape hanging off them and it gets stuck to my hair!"

The Thundercloud helmet was on the table. Megan kicked it hard. It flew out of the window and landed in the castle's cardboard recycling bin.

"Edwin! Megan! Calm down," said Minister Jill. She knew perfectly well that she couldn't say anything to help now, but all ministers know it's good to be seen doing *something*, even when it's totally and utterly pointless.

"Well I ... well I ... well I don't care if you don't want to play superheroes any more because you're a rotten Jester anyway!" said Edwin.

"And you're a rotten king! The WORST EVER!" said Megan.

"Well, you're a MASSIVE STINKY BUMFACE!" said King Edwin Flashypants.

"No! You're the MASSIVE STINKY BUMFACE!" said Megan.

Once people have called each other massive stinky bumfaces, there's really nothing more they can say.

Trying not to cry, Megan ran to the kitchen and gathered a loaf of bread and a hunk of cheese into a huge spotted handkerchief. She tied the hankie to a stick and stomped to the castle gate.

"Megan, wait. All we were doing was—" said Jill.

"I'm leaving Edwinland for ever! Goodbye, dolly murderers!"

Megan slammed the gate of Edwin's castle so hard that the shockwave knocked peasants into ditches half a mile away.

And then Megan the Jester, who had been King Edwin's faithful friend since he was a little boy, was gone.

Edwin ran to his bedroom.

He didn't want to speak to anyone.

Jill picked up the top half of the doll.

Peculiar, she thought. *The emperor could have just painted that beard on. Nobody would have minded. But it's made of lots of very small black hairs.*

Very, very peculiar.

Hairy Magic

That night, Nurbison and Globulus climbed
the steepest, most winding staircase in the
emperor's castle. Flaming torches on the walls
lit their way with a bright, steady glow.

"Oh, that's not right at all," said the
emperor. "Change the setting, Globulus!"

Globulus found a knob on the wall. He clicked it round from 'Bright, Steady Glow' to 'Dim, Spooky Flicker'.

"Much better," said the emperor, and he carried on up the stairs, stumbling a few times because he could hardly see the steps now.

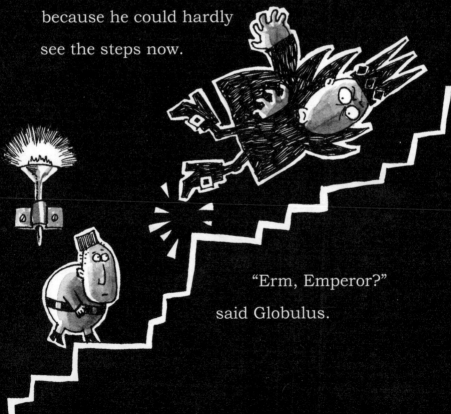

"Erm, Emperor?" said Globulus.

"You're not about to ask for something, are you, Globulus?" said Nurbison. "You know very well that I only let you ask for something every five years."

Emperor Nurbison pulled a little diary from his cloak and flicked back through the pages.

"Oh!" said the emperor, his evil eyebrow arching. "Five years, two months and three days ago: 'Globulus asks his Imperial Greatness to pass the ketchup'. So you really *are* due another. Let's get it over with, then."

"It's umm, kind of, you know, it's this," said Globulus. "There's, like, thousands of dolls of you in Edwinland now. But there's, kind of, no dolls to be helpers to them dolls. To keep all the emperor dolls company. Might be nice, yeah? Helper dolls. Sort of thing."

"Are you talking about making *Globulus* toys?" said Emperor Nurbison. "Ha! Why would anybody in the world want a toy of *you*? Oh Globulus, you are funny sometimes. You make me foo hoo hoo hoo, you really do."

Globulus knew the emperor liked his laugh to echo in a frightening way if they were on a stone staircase, so – with a sigh – he turned up the echo knob on the wall.

At last they came
to a chamber at the
top of the tower. Below
a huge window was a tiny
chair. And in the chair, Miss Dolly-Chops, the
stolen magical doll.

Half the hair was missing from her head.

"It took ages to cut off tiny bits of her magic hair, then stick it to the chins of all those dolls," said the emperor. "Used up all the glue sticks in my crafting box. But oh, it was worth it. For tonight, the moon shall be full! If my calculations are correct, Globulus – and I did once get a gold star sticker for Evil Maths at school, so they should be – the moon will rise over those hills precisely ... now!"

Emperor Nurbison and Globulus waited. No moon.

"Precisely ... now!" said the emperor, again. Still no moon.

Then the emperor remembered the clocks had gone back a couple of days before, so moonrise would be an hour later.

Nurbison and Globulus went downstairs and played some table tennis for a bit, then came up again.

"AS I WAS SAYING," said the emperor. The full moon shall rise over those hills exactly, definitely and precisely ...

... NOW!"

The chalky white circle glided over the horizon. Its cold moony beams touched the enchanted hair of Miss Dolly-Chops.

The hair began to gleam with a dazzling black light. I bet you've never seen a ray of dazzling black light before. Neither had the emperor and Globulus.

"Kind of totally wow and all of that!" said Globulus.

Miss Dolly-Chops sat up.

"I am Miss Dolly-Chops!" she said, in a voice which tinkled like a mountain stream.

"It's alive, it's alive!," said Emperor Nurbison. "The magic hair really works! Hair that I have stolen for my evil plans.

FOO HOO HOO HOO!"

"But how? My stunning locks are all here on my dainty—"

She touched her stubbly head.

"AAAAAAHHHH! MY HAAIIIRRR!"

said Miss Dolly-Chops.

"Half of it's over there in Edwinland, my dear. On the chins of a thousand dolls. Mixed in with a little bit of hair from someone else."

The emperor pulled off his false beard and stroked his bare face.

"And *that* hair will give them a certain personality ... **FOO HOO HOO!**"

Back in Edwinland, lit by the full moon, the toys came to life.

"I am Nurbison!" said one.

"I am Nurbison!" said another.

And all across the kingdom, the cry went up.

"I am Nurbison ...

I am Nurbison ...

We are Nurbison!

WE ARE NURBISON!

WE ARE NURBISON!"

So ... Many ... Nurbisons ...

All that night, King Edwin Flashypants tossed and turned. He couldn't stop thinking about Megan. He was still angry with her, but he was beginning to feel bad about the things he had said. And he was very sad that she had gone.

Well, this is a new mood, he thought. I've never felt quite this way before. I should give it a name, like *'angry-sorry'*. Or *'guilty-grumps'* or *'whoops-grrr'*.

When he finally got to sleep, he had a bad dream. He dreamt that Emperor Nurbison was standing on his chest, except Nurbison looked like an angry lollipop-lady.

When Edwin woke up, there was an angry Lollipop-Lady Nurbison doll standing on his chest.

The king pinched himself to check he really was awake. Ouch! Yes, he was.

"Your kingdom belongs to Nurbison!" said

the figure. It jabbed Edwin on the nose with the
sharp end of the lollipop, just to prove the point.

It was true. The magical toys had seized

Edwinland while everyone slept.

Centurion Alisha had put up a fight.

The trouble was, she had bought more Nurbison dolls than anyone. A Matador Nurbison had pulled down her helmet, while a Ninja Nurbison grabbed her sword. Then a Wrestler Nurbison had stamped on her toes and tripped her over. There were so many dolls that there was nothing anyone could do to stop them.

Edwinland only had one village. It was called 'Village'. And soon, an army of dolls paraded Edwin and Jill around it.

"Here is your king! Here is your minister!"
bellowed a Cricketer Nurbison to a crowd of
peasants. "They rule no more!"

"So I suppose Emperor Nurbison had
an evil plan after all," said Edwin. "Probably
something to do with the dolls being magic."

"Probably that, yes,"
said Minister Jill,
with a sigh.

Just then the real, life-sized Emperor Nurbison strode into Village. He walked very quickly, because he had written a brand-new and much faster striding theme for the marching band who followed him. The old striding theme had only got a two-star review in *Evil Ruler Monthly* magazine. Nurbison fumed for a whole week.

The emperor suddenly stopped striding – which caught the band by surprise. They all piled up behind him. Trombones crunched into banjos, which barged into bagpipes. The sound was like a whale chewing a mouthful of tin cans and fart cushions.

"Idiots of Edwinland!" said the emperor.
"You really believed that I had turned into a nice
man selling lovely toys! All part of my wicked
game, of course. With magic hair from my magic
doll, and just a sprinkle of hair
from my own beautiful face,

I knew they would come to life as little versions
of me. Just as nasty! Just as cruel! Just as keen
to seize Edwinland!

FOO HOO HOO HOO!"

All the dolls Foo hoo hoo hooed with him.

"You have done well, dolls. But I'm here
now, so *I'm* in charge. First, make me a huge
ice throne from the frozen tears of my enemies.
Then bring me an eighteen-inch pizza with a
topping of roasted baby seals. And then—"

A Beekeeper Nurbison stepped forward.

"But I am in charge! Because I am
Nurbison!" he said.

"No, I am in charge, for I am Nurbison!" said a Clown Nurbison.

Too late, the real Emperor Nurbison saw his mistake. Yes, all the toys wanted to take over Edwinland because they had the emperor's personality. He'd got that much right. But he'd missed something. Because they had his personality, every single toy wanted to be the boss.

A mob of dolls knocked the real emperor to the dusty ground.

"I am on the dusty ground!" croaked Emperor Nurbison, spitting out dust from his dusty mouth. "How dare you! I am your master, you horrid dolls!"

"Horrid *action figures*," said a Special Forces Soldier Nurbison.

"Silence!" said a Strongman Nurbison. "Now hear this! I will rule you all because I am the strongest. The clue is in the name. Strong … man. Strongman."

Wrestler Nurbison punched Strongman Nurbison into a hedge.

"No! I shall rule!" said the wrestler.

"I hardly think so," said a voice as sweet as

the sparkles on a birthday cake.

Megan's Princess Nurbison bounced forward. She was still in two pieces, but both halves of her had come to life in the night.

She fought the wrestler. Because she was in two parts, she could poke him in the eye and kick him in the bum all at the same time. And the wrestler was no match for her Pointy Hat Attack.

"*I* shall rule!" she said. "Anyone have a problem with that?"

"Err, yeah, I do," said Globulus. "There's only one proper emperor here, and he's, you know, had a lot of experience on the job, so—"

The princess booted Globulus, who landed on a compost heap.

"All hail Princess Nurbison!" shouted the toys. "ALL HAIL PRINCESS NURBISON!"

Far away, beyond Edwinland and Nurbisonia, in the jungle of Lim-Bloo-Bloo-Bloo-Bloo-Bloo-Bloo-Bloo, Megan the Jester sat on a log. She'd been walking all night in jester shoes, and her feet were tired. Jester shoes are made for prancing, not walking.

She couldn't find a name for the way she felt, but it was a lot like angry-sorry, and quite whoops-grrrr, with just a touch of guilty-grumps. It was bad of Edwin and Jill to break her doll, but Megan had thought about it for a while now, and she'd worked out they wouldn't have done it without a good reason. But Megan had been so furious she hadn't asked what that reason was.

And now I've left Edwinland, she thought, *I've nobody to jest at. If I can't be a jester, I just don't know who I am.*

A little lizard scuttled across the log. Megan had an idea.

"I'll be your jester, Lady Lizard of Lim-Bloo-Bloo-Bloo-Bloo-Bloo-Bloo-Bloo! Let the amusements begin!" Megan strummed her lute and told jokes that she thought a reptile might get.

Q: What do you call a lizard who goes moo?
A: *A cow-meleon!*

Q: What kind of snake is good at maths?
A: *An adder!*

Q: Doctor doctor! I keep thinking I'm a boa constrictor.
A: *You can't get around me like that, you know.*

The lizard blinked.

And pitter-pattered away into the trees.

"Oh dear, oh dear," said Megan. "What shall become of me?"

She picked up her stick and handkerchief, and on she walked. But with a little bit of a sniff. And a little bit of a tear.

Teamwork

"She keeps saying foo hoo hoo hoo!
That's *my* evil laugh!"

The emperor spun round.
Edwin, Jill and Globulus
ducked to avoid the drops
of water which flew from
Nurbison's fingertips.

Evil emperors never dry their hands properly after going to the toilet.

"She stole it from me! That's just evil! And being evil is fantastic, I'm not saying it isn't, but ... Oh, you know what I mean!"

The four of them had been locked in King Edwin's bedroom for ages, while Princess Nurbison decided what to do with them.

"But we've got lots of games," said Edwin. "We've got travel chess, giant chess, and chess. I don't like being locked up either, but at least my room's quite a fun place to be locked up."

"No, no, no, no, no, no!" said the emperor. "It's *my* room, just like this

is *my* castle. I claim all of Edwinland.
Haven't you learned that by now?"

Edwin put his superhero
helmet on.

SHARK
BOY SAYS
STOP BEING
SUCH A
GRUMPSTER.

Nurbison pulled the helmet
off and hurled it away. Some
ends of sticky tape were still
hanging off it, so it stuck to Globulus.

"Just for a
while, why don't we
have an Edwin half of
the room and a Nurbison
half of the room?" said
Minister Jill.

Edwin got a felt-
tip pen. He and the
emperor gripped it
together, then drew
a line across the
middle of the floor.

Both of them kept trying to push the pen to make their half bigger, so the line wobbled and zigzagged across the wooden boards.

"Oh, we're both being silly," said Edwin. "Here we are squabbling, when evil toys have taken over *both* our kingdoms. Maybe we should work together to get rid of them."

"What a horrible day this is," said the emperor. "First my enchanted dolls turn against me, then I'm locked in a bedroom, then I find myself thinking, *King Edwin's right.*"

"Your Majesty? A private word," said Minister Jill. She and Edwin went into Edwin's old playhouse. It was toddler-sized, but it

was better than
nothing.

"Work with
the Evil Emperor?"
whispered Jill.
"Who is *definitely*
still evil? Are you quite sure, Edwin?"

"Totally sure. Mostly sure. A bit sure," said
Edwin. "But you have to admit he can be very
clever. We could use his brains for a bit."

Edwin and Jill stepped out of the
playhouse. Nurbison and Globulus jumped
back, pretending they hadn't been listening at
the door.

Edwin held out his hand.

Nurbison shook it.

It was the olden days, and cameras hadn't been invented yet. So Globulus drew a very good picture of this historic moment.

"Erm, sort of, hooray, type of thing!" said Globulus.

Soon, Jill stood at Edwin's chalkboard, chalk in hand. At the top of the board, she wrote:

"Righty ho!" said Jill. "We need some ideas. Let's get creative."

King Edwin put up his hand and said, "I've got one. What about if we—"

"No," said Emperor Nurbison.

"Okay then," said Edwin. "Let's see if we can—"

"No," said Nurbison.

"Then what about—"

"No."

"Or we could—"

"No."

"We could try to—"

"No."

"Or let's—"

"No."

"Emperor, really," said Jill. "How do you know if the ideas are good or bad before you've even heard of them?"

The emperor looked at her like she was being very silly indeed.

"How can they be good ideas if it wasn't me who thought them up?" he said.

"We're going to hear each other's ideas, no matter how daft they might seem," insisted Jill.

Globulus put up his hand.

"We could, like, trap all the toys in my hat," he said.

You couldn't even fit one doll in Globulus' hat, never mind thousands. It really was the worst idea Jill had ever heard. But she had to play by her own rules, so she wrote it on the chalkboard.

Hours passed. The board filled up with ideas, ideas and more ideas. But deep down, Jill knew none of them would work.

Then Emperor Nurbison noticed something. There was still a little strip of sticky tape stuck to Globulus' nose.

Because sticky tape is almost see-through, nobody had spotted it.

"Wait, you've got sticky tape!" said the emperor. "That's useful for loads of things. Let's think about sticky tape."

Edwin ran to his superhero-costume-making table and found two rolls of tape.

"Minister Jill? Please wipe the board clean!" said King Edwin. "I think we've just had the idea. Not *an* idea. *The* idea."

A few minutes later, Jill banged on the locked bedroom door.

"What?" said the Ninja Nurbison doll on the other side.

"We request an audience with Her Majesty Princess Nurbison," said the minister.

The Princess Will See You Now

King Edwin, Emperor Nurbison, Minister Jill and Globulus walked into the throne room. A sea of Nurbison doll faces glared back at them.

Both halves of Princess Nurbison sat on Edwin's throne.

"Greetings, fools!" said the princess. "Have
you met my future wife?"

Next to the princess was a scared looking
Miss Dolly-Chops.

"That's right! We're getting married," said

the princess. "And yes, two lady dolls can get married. This is the modern world. Get used to it. Now, feeble rulers of yesteryear, what do you want?"

"We wish to proclaim you the rightful ruler of these lands," said Edwin. "Edwinland and Nurbisonia are yours forever."

"So we came to hand you our precious crowns," said the emperor.

He and Edwin took the crowns from their heads.

"All dolls in the room should make sure to get a really good look. You'll definitely want to laugh at us," said Edwin.

"Indeed," said the emperor. "So – and this is just an idea – you should probably form up into two lines. Two very long, very straight lines."

"Dolls? Form two lines!" said the princess.

"And if they stood on tall stools they'd get a really good view," said Edwin.

"Yes, stools!" said Nurbison. "Such a good idea from a child wise beyond his years."

said the princess.

Frightened peasants fetched stools for the dolls.

"And now," said the princess, "bring me the crowns."

Slowly, very slowly, Edwin and Emperor Nurbison shuffled down the middle of the hall, between the two lines of dolls – who chuckled a deep foo hoo hoo hoo. They were so busy foo hoo hoo-ing at the king and the emperor that there was something they didn't spot.

A long piece of sticky tape trailed from each of the crowns. The two bits of tape went all the way back to Globulus and Jill, who each had a roll spinning on a finger.

"Why are you walking so slowly? Get a move on!" said Princess Nurbison. But the king and the emperor couldn't risk speeding up. If the tape broke or fell off, the whole plan would be ruined.

As they neared the throne, the princess narrowed her eyes.

"Wait a minute," she said. "What's that stuck to the crowns? Is it ... sticky tape? What are you trying to—"

"Now!" said Edwin.

The king jumped to the left. The emperor jumped right. They pressed those long trails of sticky tape up against the chins of the dolls.

"**Mmmffmmmmnnpphh!**" said a surprised Ballerina Nurbison, through the tape.

"**Mmgrrrmmph!**" said a Jockey Nurbison.

"**Mmmmrrrgrrmmph!**" said a Sailor Nurbison.

"**Grmmphmmph!**" said a Funkalicious
Nurbison.

You get the idea.

"And ... throw!" said Edwin.

He and the emperor flung
their crowns high in the air ...
RIPPING away the tape from
the dolls' chins and taking all
the enchanted hair with them.
The Nurbison dolls flopped to
the ground. Without their magic
beards, they were all just ordinary
dolls again.

All except the one on the throne.

"You destroyed my army!"
screamed Princess Nurbison.
"Now you shall feel my anger!
KUNG-FU ATTACK!"

The princess's hands and feet were a blur as both halves of her jabbed and pummelled Edwin, Emperor Nurbison, Jill and Globulus into a corner of the throne room.

"POINTY-HAT ATTACK!"

said Princess Nurbison, backing into the opposite corner to get a really big run-up.

Oh no, thought Edwin. *I've seen her do this on the dolls, and they've got wooden heads. What will it do to a human being?*

The princess ran, then jumped. Her top half hurtled through the air. Straight towards King Edwin's head.

I'm finished, thought King Edwin.

"You're finished," said the emperor. "Still, rather you than me, eh?"

But, just as the pointy hat was about to strike Edwin's face, it stopped. In mid-air. Gripped by a powerful hand.

The hand of a hero.

"NOBODY hurts Shark Boy! Not when Thundercloud's around!"

Megan! There she was, wearing her Thundercloud helmet. She'd rescued it from the cardboard recycling bin, so there were loads of rotten banana skins stuck to it. No matter how many times Jill asked, people always threw the

wrong rubbish in the wrong hole. But stinky
banana peel or not, Edwin couldn't be more glad
to see her.

"You came back!" said Edwin. "What happened, right, is the toys all had magic hair in their beards and they came to life and took over and Emperor Nurbison thought they would obey him but they didn't and then— Hey, how about I tell you the whole thing later, after we've won? If we win. Let's try to win first."

"Let me go! LET ME GO!" the princess yelled.

Megan was holding the top half of the princess like an ice-cream cornet, but an ice-cream cornet with fists and snapping teeth. Meanwhile, her bottom half was kicking Megan in the shins.

"Shark Boy to the rescue!" said Edwin. He scrambled up Megan's back, peeled a piece of sticky tape from her cardboard helmet, slapped it on the doll's chin, and ripped it away.

And Princess Nurbison was just a happy smiling broken-in-half doll again.

Edwin and Megan hugged like two koalas.

"Megan, you're my best chum in the world!" said Edwin.

"Can I be your jester again?" said Megan. "I thought up a new joke.

How do you keep cool at a football match? You stand next to a fan!"

Everybody laughed, even Emperor Nurbison. But he wasn't laughing in the nice way.

"FOO HOO HOO HOO! This is just the beginning!"

"Here we go," said Minister Jill.

Nurbison grabbed Miss Dolly-Chops from the throne.

"She's still got plenty of hair, and my beard will soon grow back! I shall make new dolls! And *this* time I'll fix them so they obey me! And with my invincible legions of dolls I shall—"

Miss Dolly-Chops was torn from the emperor's grasp.

"So that's where she is!" said old Empress Veronica. "What do you think you're doing, Nurbison? Stealing from your own mother! A frail, helpless old lady!"

The frail, helpless old lady got the emperor in a headlock.

"I'm – I'm sorry Mum ..." whimpered Emperor Nurbison.

"Sorry's not good enough!" said the empress.
"I'm going to drag you home by the nose and spank
you with a candlestick. A spiky candlestick."

She felt around his face for a few minutes.
There was no sign of a nose at all. He just didn't
seem to have one.

"Well, an ear will do," said
Veronica. "OW!
OW.
OWW!"

said the emperor,
as his mum
hauled him away.

What We've All Learned

After every adventure, King Edwin and all his friends would gather on the village green to talk about what they'd learned. So when all the Nurbison dolls had been cleared away, that's just what they did.

First, one of the peasants stood up.

"We peasants have learned something," she said. "We've learned not to buy toys from evil emperors. From now on we will only get them from recognised toy outlets with good safety standards."

Minister Jill stood up.

"I've learned something," said Minister Jill. "I've learned that to get the job done, sometimes we need to work with people we don't always like. Also, I learned that King Edwin is the cleverest and bravest king there is. But I sort of knew that already."

Centurion Alisha stood up.

"I've learned that we palace guards need to be better at defending this kingdom," said Alisha. "We've let it get invaded a couple of times now. That's embarrassing. Look at me. This is my embarrassed face."

Everybody looked at Alisha. Her embarrassed face looked just the same as her angry face, or her happy face.

Baxter the Hermit would have stood up at about this time, but he was still in the kitchen, upside down in a pot, pretending to be a plant.

Then King Edwin and Megan the Jester stood up together.

"We've learned something really big!" said Megan. "We've learned that even the best of friends can sometimes make each other sad."

"But if they make up," said Edwin, "they can be best friends all over again!"

"And what's more ..." said Megan.

Everyone waited for her to finish. But she couldn't think of anything extra to say. So she did a dance. Then she fell over. The people laughed and cheered.

"Now let's *all* play superheroes!" said Megan.

And everybody did ...

FOOTSIE

PROFESSOR STRIPER

ULTIMATE MINISTER

HARE KID

DEERSK8R

EQUUS

NORSE FELLER

SHARK BOY

THE HUMAN MAN

THAT MONKEY

GYMNASTICA

SUPERSHINYHEAD

POWER HAMSTER

That night, as Globulus went to bed in his tiny room in the emperor's castle, clutching a mug of cold spider's milk, he heard a sharp knock.

"Kind of, like, I suppose, umm, sort of, I guess, I reckon, sort of, umm, yeah, like, you know, errr, so, kind of, like, I suppose, umm, errr, well, kind of, like, so, errr, well, you know, come in," said Globulus, but Emperor Nurbison had already flung the door open.

"Globulus!" said the emperor. "I really don't know why I did this, but I made you a doll of my handsome self."

He delved into his flapping cloak and pulled out a little Nurbison doll.

"It isn't magic. Mother has all the magic hair now. But here it is anyway. And with it, this."

Nurbison placed a little Globulus doll next to it.

"Wow, like, a matching set!" said Globulus, "You and me! That's like, kind of amazing, and sort of just what I wanted, and thank you."

"Now sleep," said the emperor. "You have to get up and work for me again in half an hour."

The emperor left Globulus, then prowled through the dark passages of his castle, back to his own room.

Then he stopped. And thought.

I just gave Globulus a present. I did something nice for someone. How did that happen? That's not me. I never do anything nice for anybody. I am the Evil Emperor!

Then he worked it out. All those weeks of pretending to be nice had changed him, ever so slightly. There was now a tiny, intsy-wintsy bit of good in him.

"Well, you mutant part of me that is good, I shall defeat you!" spat Nurbison. "Yes I shall! By becoming even more evil than ever before! SQUEE HEE H — ahem, I mean FOO HOO HOO HOO!"

In Edwinland, King Edwin was going to bed, too. Playing superheroes had made him super-tired. Minister Jill tucked him in.

"I've had a lot of surprises on our

adventures, Jill," said the young king. "But none as big as the first time I saw a *living doll*."

"You sleep now, Edwin," said Jill.

"Toys that come to life!" said Edwin, yawning. "Can you imagine a bigger surprise than that? I can't. And I've got a big imagination. Any time my imagination doesn't feel big enough, I just imagine it's a bit bigger, and then, ta-daa! It really is."

"Night night," said Jill.

"But Jill, you never said if you could imagine a bigger— "

But she was already gone.

In the hallway, Minister Jill looked through a window to the moonlit ocean far away. She *could* think of something that would surprise Edwin even more than dolls that come to life. But she had never told anyone about it.

What is Jill's secret?

We will find out.

In another book.

The End

Ask Globulus

YOUR PROBLEMS, SOLVED!

Q *Dear Globulus*

I have to wear glasses, but every pair of glasses I buy breaks when I hit it twelve times with a massive hammer. What can I do?

A Hi, umm, maybe you could try, you know, not hitting them twelve times with a massive hammer. Cut down to three or four times, yeah? And if you still got the problem then maybe ... you know … try not hitting them with the hammer. Like, ever. Sounds mad, I know, but give it a go, sort of thing.

Q Dear Globulus

I grow lettuce in my garden but the slugs keep eating them in the night. How can I stop them?

A Slugs, yeah? Yeah. Thing about slugs is, they're not very good at, you know, jumping. Ever see a slug jump? No. Me neither. So I reckon, right, you should kind of like put in a line of hurdles in front of the lettuce patch, and there's like no way a slug is going to clear more than one of them. Hurdling slugs. Not going to happen.

Or you could eat the slugs. Bit slimy, sure, but no worse than worms and, you know, we all eat worms, don't we.

Q Dear Globulus

My brother won't let me play with his football. What can I do?

A You're sort of going, "I want the ball," yeah, and your brother, he's going, "I want the ball." But you got to think, yeah, about what the ball wants. Let the ball choose. And maybe you think balls don't have a mind and can't choose, but that's when you've got to draw a face on the ball, okay? Cause, you know, if you draw a face on something then you give it a mind. That's how it works. Pretty sure anyway. I once drew a face on my own face, yeah? And that sort of gave me an extra mind and my brain got double clever. Wait, what were we talking about?

Q *Globulus!*
Why are you still answering letters?
I need a custard cream biscuit! ***NOW!***

A Hello Emperor. Sorry Emperor. Coming Emperor.

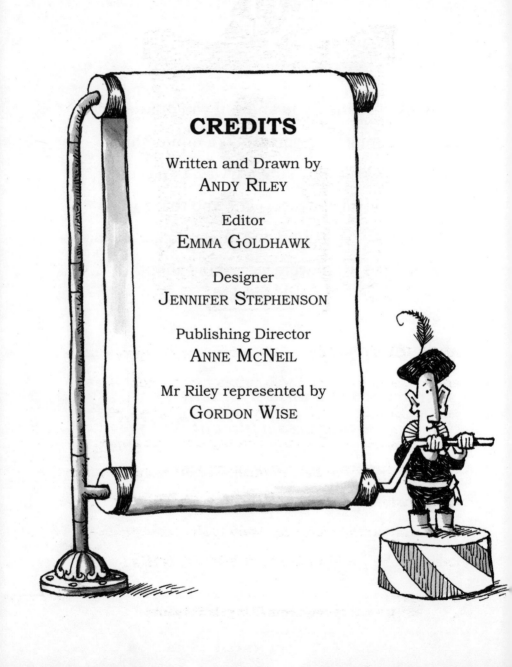

CREDITS

Written and Drawn by
ANDY RILEY

Editor
EMMA GOLDHAWK

Designer
JENNIFER STEPHENSON

Publishing Director
ANNE MCNEIL

Mr Riley represented by
GORDON WISE

ANDY RILEY

ANDY RILEY has done lots of funny writing for film and TV, and he's even won prizes for it, like BAFTAs and an Emmy. For TV, Andy co-wrote the scripts for David Walliams's *Gangsta Granny* and *The Boy In The Dress*, and *Robbie the Reindeer*. The films he's written for include *Gnomeo and Juliet* and *The Pirates! In an Adventure with Scientists*. Andy really loves cowboy hats and he can do a brilliant FOO HOO HOO.

www.facebook.com/KingFlashypants